Betty's New Best Friend

A tale of two coos

Written by Jayne Baldwin

Illustrated by Caroline Smith

To:
Jack & James,

With love,

Grandma
&
Grandpa

In a wee part o' Scotland
where the hills meet the sea

There's a stripy sort of cow
that's called a Beltie

They have curly black coats,
and are chunky and round

With white striped tums
almost reaching
the ground.

Betty the Beltie
wanted to play
but everyone
seemed to be
busy today.

The bees were buzzing,
the rabbits were crabbit,
the hedgehogs were hibernating
which is their habit.

Sheep were being shorn
and the chickens
were broody,

And on top of that
Betty's brother
was moody.

Betty wandered away leaving the herd behind,
wondering if there was some fun she could find.

She cropped at the grass,
and looked at the sky,
and watched as the wispy
white clouds floated by.

**Amongst some trees
the wood mice
were napping**

**and the
golden pheasant
was squawking
and flapping.**

Chit chats were chittering,
and sparrows were bickering,
and high in the sky
a tiny lark was twittering.

Then over the dyke
and through a small wood,
Betty caught sight
of a hairy thing stood.

She could not believe
what was in front of her eyes,
was this a Belted Galloway in disguise?

She had to stop,
to think and stare,
she'd never seen anything
with so much hair!

It was like a great
big ginger mound,
standing quite still,
not making a sound.

She didn't know whether
to laugh or be scared,
whatever it was didn't
belong to her herd.

The big scruffy beast then lifted its head.
"What sort of thing are you?" Betty said.

You're so red
like a squirrel,
a deer
or a fox.

But I've never seen anything with such luscious locks.

"I can moo like you"
a voice came back,
just because I'm not
white and black."

"But your heads got things
sticking out at the side!"
"These are my horns"
the young bull said with pride.

I'm from the herd of Highlands over the way,
I was bored and wondered if someone would play.
I'm really happy to find someone new,
my name is Archie, lovely to meet you.

I'm Betty the Beltie
from beyond that peak,
would you like to play with me?
Hide and seek?

Archie said "yes
shall I count up to ten?
And then when I've found you,
we'll start over again".

Can you find Betty?
Where should
Archie hide?

It's going to be tricky to keep
his horns out of sight!

Do you think you'd like
to play hide and seek?
I'll count to ten,
promise not to peek.

One, two, three, four, five, six,
seven, eight, nine, ten!
Coming ready or not!

The moral rights of the author and illustrator have been asserted in accordance with the Copyright, Designs and Patents Act 1988.
ISBN: 978-1-8380-3790-1
Published by Foggie Toddle Books
18 North Main Street, Wigtown DG8 9HL
01988 402896
hello@foggietoddlebooks.co.uk